GUARDIANS OF EGYPT

PHIL PHILIPS

Requests to publish work from this book should be sent to:
admin@philphilips.com

Philips, Phil, 1978-

ISBN-13: 978-0-6482724-4-1
ISBN-10: 0-6482724-4-3

Typeset in Sabon

For more information visit
www.philphilips.com

Dedicated to my fans

BOOK BLURB

When Julien Bonnet finds the remains of an ancient city under the Red Sea, he unleashes the might of the Guardians of Egypt. They carry the burden of destroying ancient sites – and anyone who discovers them – to keep their secret safe.

Only this time, they messed with the wrong guy. Killing him will not be as simple as it seems.

AUTHOR'S NOTE

General Julien Bonnet is a mysterious character we love, but know little about, in Mona Lisa's Secret and the Last Secret Chamber.

The reason why he has a scar on his face and why he opened his heart and asked teenager, Boyce, to join his special unit team will be answered in this short story.

Chapter 1

Outside of Cairo, Egypt

British archaeologist Damien Brey and his wife, Elizabeth, broke through the rubble to enter a tomb that had been sealed for thousands of years. The foul trapped air that escaped the entrance made them both reach for their noses in disgust. They crawled into the narrow cavity that opened up into a vast space. Dust motes floated in the air as their flashlights circled the void covered in what looked to be ape bones piled up against one another. There was no sarcophagus or ancient treasure, but a church-like chamber coated in primate skulls that was framed by four solid pillars that ran upward to an arched ceiling.

'What is this place?' Elizabeth asked, stopping to study the imagery etched into the stone walls by skilled stonemasons.

'The writing is not ancient Egyptian,' said Damien, taking it all in as he rubbed the wall with his right hand. 'Some sort of Pre-dynastic, ancient civilization, maybe.'

'Look at these elongated heads.' Elizabeth pointed. 'They look creepy.'

'That was not uncommon in ancient Egypt. Pharaoh Akhenaten was known to have a large oval head,' answered Damien, following the limestone to his right, as Elizabeth moved in the opposite direction.

'Some of these drawings look like alien spacecraft.'

'Yes, I noticed that too.'

'So, the million-dollar question is ...' Elizabeth paused for dramatic effect, 'who were these people who built this place and why the burial site for monkeys? I know falcons and cats were held in the highest esteem in ancient Egypt, but never monkeys.'

'Look here,' said Damien, inspecting the mural that ran the entire length of the room. 'It looks like they were being trained to farm the lands. There are hundreds of apes with pickaxes, while the men with the unusually long heads watched on.'

'I've never seen anything like this before.'

'Me neither.'

Damien paused to study a symbol then stopped dead in his tracks. It was an image that was recognized throughout the modern twentieth century. 'It can't be,' he murmured, bringing Elizabeth's attention back to him.

'What is it?'

'They were test monkeys.'

'What?' She frowned.

'Doesn't this symbol over here look like a DNA helix?'

Elizabeth moved to examine the image in question. 'You're scaring me now,' she said breathlessly. 'What in the hell did we discover?'

Damien glanced with trepidation into his wife's

brown eyes. 'I think this is telling our story,' he said slowly, hardly daring to believe it. 'Our history, how our species came to be evolved from ... Homo Erectus to Homo Sapiens. My God, Elizabeth,' he breathed. 'The images are saying it clearly.'

All of a sudden, the sound of rocks being crushed beneath feet filtered through from the outside cave.

Damien and Elizabeth turned to the entrance to see three men standing just outside the chamber through the small opening. They were dressed in white thobes and modern-day sneakers, but the sunlight behind them made it impossible to make out their faces. They spoke in Arabic and the words echoed around the Brits inside the chamber.

'Hello, who's out there?' asked Elizabeth, ensuring she sounded warm and friendly.

There was no answer.

'We are archaeologists from the University of Cambridge and we have permits to study this site,' said Damien, quietly nervous. He knew that even though he had permits, these lands were considered dangerous and Egyptians didn't like the way international nations were researching their desert like it was their own. This wouldn't be the first time he'd had incidents with the locals, and on many dangerous occasions he'd had to give them money to keep them away.

'We are the Guardians of Egypt,' said a man in deeply accented English. 'You have discovered a secret that will never be allowed to be shared with the world.'

'What do you mean?' Damien said out loud,

approaching the entrance. 'Hang on, I'm coming out, this is just a misunderstanding.'

'Stay there!' said the stranger.

'I'm sure we can work this out. I will pay you.'

'*Yalla! Yalla!*' Damien heard the men say.

Elizabeth grabbed onto her husband's shoulders, clearly frightened. Quiet ensued for a brief moment.

'I'm sorry,' the man said. 'I really am.'

Four grenades were tossed inside the cavity. They bounced around aimlessly, coming to a stop around the couple's feet.

'No, wait!' Elizabeth cried, her body shaking in terror.

'Holly shit!' Damien muttered, knowing this would be the last place he would ever see. He turned to his wife and drew her into his arms.

Boom!

The entire cave collapsed on top of itself, eliminating the archaeologists and the past from existence.

One of the white-robed men left behind a symbol with a black spray can on the outside wall, which was later to become known as the mark of the Guardians.

Chapter 2

Outside of Cairo, Egypt

Thirty-year-old Julien Bonnet found the fishing boat that was to take him to a dive site yet to be explored by man. A teenager who discovered the site claimed to have found the remains of an ancient city. Approaching the vessel from the long timber jetty on Naama Bay, a group of men congregated nearby around an expensive moored speedboat.

The boy's name was Ezra, and his smile was infectious as he greeted Julien onboard with an over-enthusiastic handshake. The boy's father, Saad, was waiting by the steering wheel with a wide grin. The family resemblance was uncanny and they seemed to be genuine, honest people. It was evident that the money they were going to make on this diving adventure was going to help them raise the funds needed to compete with a plethora of diving companies already active within the region, and Julien wanted to help them.

'Two hundred US dollars now,' said Julien, handing over the cash to the father. 'Another five hundred if this site your son is bragging about is real. If I'm not impressed you get nothing else.'

'You won't regret it,' said Ezra, directing him to take a seat. 'Like I told you when we met the other day, this site is not like any other I've ever seen. There are large statues, pillars and tablets with intact images of alien heads that you must see.'

'I'm looking forward to it.'

The men on the jetty gave Julien and his party a cold stare. As he was an experienced captain in the French army, Julien had noticed their prying eyes instantly, but he excused it as jealousy and relaxed himself into his cushioned leather seat. Ezra detached the mooring ropes, Saad pushed the throttle forward and the boat drifted away in the direction of the Red Sea.

'We never did find out what you do for a living and why you're in Egypt,' asked Saad at the wheel, who had shoved the Benjamin Franklins into his pants pocket. 'As soon as Ezra found out that you too loved to dive, the conversation became one-sided. He gets so passionate about the sea and you can't shut him up when he gets started.'

Julien flashed the teen a smile. 'I share the same passion. I totally understand the thrill of diving in the deep sea,' replied Julien, turning to face Ezra, whose eyes were glued to Julien. 'I'm actually on vacation. I always wanted to come dive here. I hear it's the best in the world.'

Ezra nodded his head and moved to a storage cabinet nearby.

'I work for the government,' said Julien.

Ezra grinned, most probably thinking Julien sat on a desk and pushed papers all day. A man with deep pockets. What he wouldn't know was that Julien was one of the most decorated officers within the French intelligence with a track record of zero failure. If a group of terrorists or an organization threatened France, he was the man they called to eliminate the problem.

The fishing boat sliced through the water, while Ezra dumped the heavy diving equipment on the blue carpeted floor between them.

'There are only two sets. You're not coming down?' Julien jokingly asked the driver; the man bore an enormous beer belly.

'Not in a million years,' he replied. 'A captain always stays with his boat.'

'Totally understand. How long till we reach the destination?'

'One hour.'

The Egyptian summer sun splayed across the perfectly calm Red Sea, considered to be one of the seven wonders of the underwater world. Its name was taken from the periodic algal blooms that occurred here, which painted the sea with a reddish hue, rather than the red-tinted Egyptian mountain ranges that surrounded it.

Julien and Ezra suited up, both gave the OK signal and stepped off the back of the boat into the warm waters of the Red Sea. The visibility was amazingly crystal clear, but as they continued their descent toward the ruins, they switched on the torches to give them extra clarity.

Equalizing and finding neutral buoyancy, Ezra led the way along the sea floor. An eerie red caused by the algae refracting the light from above made the shadows seem much larger as they hovered over the sandy bedrock.

A temple suddenly loomed out of nowhere.

Julien initially fought to hold in a smile, but it was impossible and he succumbed to the beauty before him. Massive pillars that were half-buried in silt framed what appeared to be an enormous underwater site that had been lost in time. Colossal decapitated heads of Pharaoh Akhenaten and his queen, Nefertiti, stood prominent in an area where giant tablets lined up against one another. To see their long faces beneath the Red Sea caused a shiver to run up Julien's spine. Akhenaten was not just any pharaoh. He was Tutankhamun's father and he ruled for seventeen years during the eighteenth dynasty, during which time he broke away from the worship of multiple pagan Gods to a single monotheistic deity, the son god, Aten, who was later adopted by the Christian church.

Julien took in a deep breath of air. This was what Ezra had been bragging about.

As they approached the tablets around the rocky reef, a school of blue spotted stingray suddenly appeared out of the dark and sped right by them. Julien reacted with haste and avoided the poisonous spines at the base of their extremely long tails that brushed past him. He relaxed his breathing, regaining his focus, and reached the tablets in question.

At first sight, Julien could tell the markings were not Egyptian hieroglyphs. He ran his fingers through the grooves in the stone with his gloved hand. The elongated heads depicted in the tablets were obviously referencing Akhenaten and Nefertiti, whose heads lay feet away.

Thousands of monkey-like animals were pictured farming and holding pickaxes. On one enormous tablet was the god Aten in the form of a bright sun. In its center was another round image where Osiris, the God of the Dead and ruler of the underworld, was pictured as a falcon-headed man exiting its core.

Ezra pointed to the image and signaled the OK sign, as if to say, 'I told you so.'

Julien nodded his head and mock-punched the teen in the shoulder to show he had done well to find this place, and Julien would pay the five hundred he'd promised at the beginning of the trip.

Moments later, a speedboat with a fire-engine-red-framed body stopped and hovered above them. Julien grew still, all traces of fun evaporating. It was the same boat the men on the jetty had surrounded. The same men with hatred in their eyes.

Chapter 3

Muffled gun shots could be heard below sea level. Ezra panicked and a plume of bubbles escaped his mouth as he began to frantically kick his legs. Julien kept the regulator in Ezra's mouth and tried to keep him still and calm. The rhythmic sound of breathing intensified for the both of them as they knelt on the seabed and waited.

Who were these guys and did they just kill Ezra's father?

No sooner had Julien asked the question than something heavy entered the water.

It was Ezra's father, who had been gunned down and tossed out to sea like he was nothing. His body spread-eagled and floated on the surface for a couple of seconds, before slowly sinking to his grave beneath the sea he so admired and loved.

Rage erupted within Julien, but he needed to tamp it down for now. He had to take control of the situation and protect the teenager, who had lost the most important person in his life. He could see tears of anguish through Ezra's face mask. Julien comforted the kid with an embrace and checked his diving watch. They still had enough air and needed to wait it out in the hope that the murderers above would leave the scene.

At that moment, anchored brick-sized objects entered the water all around them, falling in all directions.

Julien's eyes widened with fear. As one dropped behind Ezra, Julien realized they were explosive devices. He tried to yank the teen away to safety, but it was too late.

The bombs erupted. One after the other they exploded and the underwater world got turned upside down.

Ezra was pushed with incredible pressure to the seabed and collided with the ground, his scuba-gear mask and breathing apparatus smashed in two. Julien tried to reach him, but the boy was sucked into a whirlpool of currents and pulled in the opposite direction, his body growing still and drifting out of Julien's line of sight, never to be seen again.

Julien was forced around like a rag doll, spinning in a mist of grey bubbles as the ancient site crumbled all around him. His chest collided with a solid surface – he was pinned to the ground and the pressure was driving the air from his lungs. He realized the solid structure was a broken piece from Akhenaten's decapitated head. He dug his fingers into the grooves as his body was thrust upward with the next explosion. Debris of crushed rocks came flying at his face with intensity and connected with hefty blows across his head. All he could do was hang on as blow after blow slammed into him.

The water was now a red hue all around him. His

regulator was smashed, making his breathing erratic, but it still seemed to be operational.

Pain lashed through him, but he continued to hold on tight until the arsenal of bombs had been depleted. What felt like an eternity later but was in fact only seconds, the waters once again were calm and he found himself kneeling on the seabed with his head raised upward.

The speedboat roared its powerful engines and disappeared out of sight.

Julien slowly ascended, stopping to decompress for a couple of minutes, and hoping that his blood would not attract the sharks. He saw Saad's fishing boat sink only meters away. As it overturned in the water, he noticed there was a new symbol across the deckhouse, marked with a black spray can. Julien clenched his fists. He'd seen that mark before on the news. These terrorists were responsible for blowing up countless ancient sites throughout Egypt these past couple of years, as more sites were being discovered. They had managed to fly under the radar until now.

Julien exited the water gasping for breath, and grabbing hold of a broken piece of timber he saw amongst the remaining rubble, he began to kick in the direction of land. His young friend and his father had been murdered under his protection and the only thought that flooded his mind was to avenge their tragic deaths.

The Guardians of Egypt would not know it yet, but they were up against a madman the French intelligence had nicknamed 'the plague'. Every mission he commanded never ended well for the other side. It was only a matter of time before they felt his wrath.

Chapter 4

After two long hours of kicking to shore, Julien was picked up by two local fishermen doing their rounds. He slumped on the bench seat, fatigued, and shut his eyes to take a breath while the blood gushed out of his face.

A towel was immediately handed over so he could apply pressure to his wounded temple. It smelled like fish, but Julien wasn't complaining.

One of the men asked him a question in Arabic.

Julien answered, 'Sorry, I only speak French and English.'

'Yes, we speak English,' said the older of the two. 'You will need stitches, it's a deep cut.'

'Yep.'

'What happened to you?'

'My boat sank.'

The old man laughed and relayed the information to his friend, who also laughed. 'You're lucky the sharks didn't kill you from all that blood.'

Julien thanked the men for their help and they assured him he was in good hands and would take him to the Sharm International Hospital once they arrived to shore.

* * *

After a long day that ended with Julien getting stitched up, he proceeded to his hotel suite at the Royal Savoy and crashed on his bed. The events that had transpired today ran over in his mind as he stared up at the ceiling fan. The irony in all this, he thought, was that he had traveled to a remote place to holiday and dive the seas, to escape the madness that was his job, and it somehow still had found him.

After some much-needed shut-eye, he woke up fresh and with a new objective: to find these assholes.

Day one on the search turned into day two and three. He searched for the red speedboat everywhere but came up empty every time. The men seemed to have vanished.

One entire week flew by with no results.

On the eighth day, Julien was enjoying a nice meal overlooking a lively shopping strip filled with restaurants and cafes. A couple of girls, most likely tourists, flirted with him, giggling amongst themselves. Julien turned his face purposely to show the distinctive scar he had obtained days ago, to scare off the girls, and it seemed to have worked as their smiles disappeared and they left him alone.

He finished his meal and headed for his hired Mustang. It was dark and the air was warm and the street was brimming with people. At his driver's window he noticed a reflection of a boat. His head swung as if in slow motion to see the red speedboat he'd been searching for all this time, sitting on a trailer behind a black SUV.

Julien reacted swiftly and tailgated the boat,

managing to keep his distance so as not to be seen. It led him to a luxury villa with tall front gates. He parked his vehicle down the street and entered the neighbour's front yard, giving him easy access to jump the fence into an amazing landscaped garden. Palm trees lit up by spotlights framed the driveway that led to an enormous property rendered in an orange brown.

He stayed in the shadows and found himself an open window to climb through, which led him into a study. The smell of lacquered timber perfumed the room as he snooped around the desk. A glass-framed poster was up on the wall depicting the symbol he had come to know and hate.

Julien was unarmed, but it didn't worry him. This wouldn't be the first time he needed to kill with his bare hands. Entering the hallway, he could hear men talking while playing a game of snooker; the distinctive sound of balls clattered around the green baize as he edged closer. Julien peeked into the billiard room to check for any signs of danger, making sure no guns were present before casually strolling in to join them.

The look on their faces was priceless.

Eyes widened with fear. Words in Arabic were spoken urgently and by their reaction it seemed like they recognized him.

'Yes, I survived,' Julien said coldly, his hands balled into fists. 'You killed two friends of mine.'

'I think you're mistaken,' said the oldest man in broken English, taking a step back.

'You left me scarred, this I will never forgive you for.'

Two of the men held onto pool cues while the

other extracted a pocket knife, but it didn't concern Julien in the slightest. It made him smile; he lived for this shit.

Julien stepped forward, his towering height making him loom like a giant over the shorter Middle Eastern men.

The first cue swung at his head. Julien ducked and weaved, avoiding the blow, and answered back with a quick jab square in the man's nose, sending him bleeding onto the tiled floor.

More words of hatred and anguish were thrown in Arabic. Julien continued to move forward like a boxer, never backing down.

The man with the knife came at him hard and in a blocking, swooping motion Julien managed to grab the man's hand and drive the knife back into his heart, killing him instantly. Sneakily, the man with the bleeding nose jumped at the opportunity and wrapped the cue around Julien's neck. A strong elbow in the man's rib cage released his grip, and as Julien turned he came down strong with the palm of his hand and snapped the cue in half. Extracting one of the broken pieces, he stabbed the man in the neck before he even had a chance to move.

Two men brutally killed, one man still remained.

The coward hid behind the pool table, holding onto his cue stick.

'You don't understand,' he said, fear written all over his face. 'We're the good guys. The Guardians are the keepers who protect a secret that's been hidden for thousands of years.'

Julien extracted the bloody cue from the dead

man's carotid artery and approached the last man standing, who ran in the opposite direction around the table. 'What secret are you protecting?' asked Julien, his voice stony.

The old man shook his head, as if to say he would never tell.

'You fucked with the wrong guy, now you must suffer the consequence.'

Moving around the table, the old man decided to make a run for it in his plush backyard. Hot on his tail, Julien grabbed him by the neck and plunged his head inside a pond where dolphins spat out water from their mouths.

'I'll tell you,' the man pleaded, breaking his head out of the water for a split second before being pushed right back under.

At that moment the sound of the water and the bubbles escaping his mouth reminded Julien of the young boy who had died deep within the Red Sea. That child would never be able to grow, start a family, and do the things he was passionate about.

The emotion and anger overwhelmed him.

'Keep your secret,' Julien said with gritted teeth, suffocating the man until his body went limp.

The so-called Guardians of Egypt had been eliminated by a man who would one day become the general of the French intelligence, and part of a team that would include another teenage boy, and they would discover unimaginable treasures, including the secret these men had kept till their dying breath.

ACKNOWLEDGMENTS

I want to thank my beautiful wife Marie, and my two boys Alexander and Leonardo who continue to support me throughout this amazing journey.

A big thank you to my extended family, parents and friends for their loving support and always believing in me.

A special thank you goes out to my editor Alexandra Nahlous for giving this short story life.

Last of all to you, my dear reader, for picking up my book. I truly hope you have as much fun reading it as I did writing it. I would love to hear from you. I can be contacted via social media, or on my website **philphilips.com**

ABOUT THE AUTHOR

Also by Amazon Best Selling Author Phil Philips.

- Mona Lisa's Secret
- Last Secret Chamber
- Fortune in Blood

Phil Philips writing style has been linked to Dan Brown and Matthew Reilly.

View the Cinematic Book Trailers to all my novels and join me on Social Media.

Sign up to join my Reader's Group and you'll receive a free chapter to one of my novels. You also will be notified on give-aways and upcoming new releases.

Mona Lisa's Secret

Joey is the great-grandson of Vincenzo Peruggia, the man who stole the original Mona Lisa in 1911. Along with his girlfriend, Marie, an art connoisseur, he stumbles across his father's secret room, and finds himself staring at what he thinks is a replica of da Vinci's most famous masterpiece.

BUT IT IS NO FAKE ...

The Louvre has kept this secret for over one hundred years, waiting for the original to come to light, and now they want it back at any cost.

With Marie held hostage and the Louvre curator and his men hot on his trail, Joey is left to run for his life in an unfamiliar city, with the priceless Mona Lisa his only bargaining chip. While formulating a plan to get Marie back with the help from an unexpected quarter, Joey discovers hidden secrets within the painting, secrets which, if made public, could change the world forever.

In this elaborately plotted, fast-paced thriller, Phil Philips takes you on a roller-coaster ride through the streets of Paris and to the Jura mountains of Switzerland, to uncover a secret hidden for thousands of years ...

Last Secret Chamber

WHERE IS THE LAST SECRET CHAMBER OF ANCIENT EGYPT, AND WHAT DOES IT HIDE?

When an archaeologist is murdered in his Egyptian apartment, an ancient artefact is stolen from his safe, one believed to hold the clue to the last secret chamber.

When Joey Peruggia discovers the dead man was his long-lost uncle, he travels with his girlfriend, Marie, and his friend Boyce, who works for the French intelligence, to Egypt, on a mission to find the answers to the murder.

But once they arrive, they are lured into a trap and become hostages to a crazed man and his gang of thieves. A man who would stop at nothing to discover what lies in the last secret chamber.

All bets are off, and only the cleverest will survive this deadliest of adventures.

In this elaborately plotted, fast-paced thriller, Phil Philips takes you on a roller-coaster ride through Egypt's most adored structures on the Giza plateau, to uncover a secret hidden for thousands of years ...

Fortune in Blood

A NOVEL OF MURDER, THEFT, BETRAYAL AND
MONEY ... LOTS OF IT ...

Joey used to be a carefree surfer kid on Venice Beach. But as
the youngest son of a notorious gangster, it seems he can't
escape the life. Soon he's forced to prove himself by leading a
team in the heist of the century. Will he be able to pull it off?

Vince was always worried about getting to lectures on time
... and spending time with his hot girlfriend. But everything
changes when he's embroiled in his detective father's world.
Now he's on the run for his life from the mob.

FBI Agent Monica is smart, beautiful, tough and unyielding.
Caught in the middle of the mob and the police, her loyalty
is being questioned by both sides. But Monica seems to have
her own agenda ... In a world where corruption is rife, she
will be tested to the limit.

Who can be trusted and who will be left standing? And who
will ultimately escape with all the money? A showdown is set
in motion and no one will be left unscathed.

*In this elaborately plotted, fast-paced thriller, Phil Philips
takes you on a roller coaster ride that will keep you guessing
until the very last page.*

ONE MORE THING ...

If you loved the book and have a moment to spare, I would really appreciate a short review where you bought the book. Your help in spreading the word is gratefully appreciated.